THE FARMER IN THE DELL

illustrated by

ALEXANDRA WALLNER

Holiday House/New York

For Adèle Bernhard—
Wishing you love, peace, joy always

A.W.

Illustrations copyright © 1998 by Alexandra Wallner
ALL RIGHTS RESERVED
Printed in the United States of America
FIRST EDITION

Library of Congress Cataloging-in-Publication Data
Wallner, Alexandra.
The farmer in the dell / by Alexandra Wallner. — 1st ed.
p.   cm.
Summary: An illustrated version of the traditional game song
accompanied by music.
ISBN 0-8234-1382-9
1. Folk songs, English—United States—Texts.   [1. Folk songs—
United States.   2. Singing games.   3. Games.]   I. Title.
PZ8.3.W18Far   1998   97-44206   CIP   AC
782.42162'13'00268—dc21

The farmer in the dell, the farmer in the dell,

Hi ho, the derrio,

the farmer in the dell.

The farmer takes a wife,

the farmer takes a wife,

Hi ho, the derrio,

the farmer takes a wife.

The wife takes a child, the wife takes a child,

Hi ho, the derrio, the wife takes a child.

The child takes a nurse,

the child takes a nurse,

Hi ho, the derrio,

the child takes a nurse.

The nurse takes a dog,

the nurse takes a dog,

Hi ho, the derrio,

the nurse takes a dog.

The dog takes a cat, the dog takes a cat,

Hi ho, the derrio, the dog takes a cat.

The cat takes a rat, the cat takes a rat,

Hi ho, the derrio, the cat takes a rat.

The rat takes a cheese,

the rat takes a cheese…

Hi ho, the derrio,

the rat takes a cheese.

The cheese stands alone, the cheese stands alone,

Hi ho, the derrio, the cheese stands alone.

THE FARMER IN THE DELL

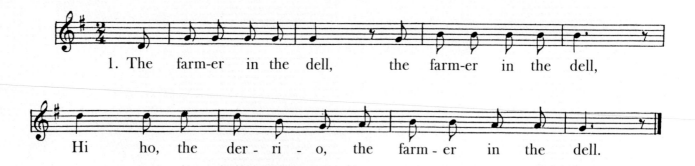

1. The farm-er in the dell, the farm-er in the dell,
Hi ho, the der - ri - o, the farm - er in the dell.

2. The farmer takes a wife, the farmer takes a wife,
   Hi ho, the derrio, the farmer takes a wife.

3. The wife takes a child, the wife takes a child,
   Hi ho, the derrio, the wife takes a child.

4. The child takes a nurse, the child takes a nurse,
   Hi ho, the derrio, the child takes a nurse.

5. The nurse takes a dog, the nurse takes a dog,
   Hi ho, the derrio, the nurse takes a dog.

6. The dog takes a cat, the dog takes a cat,
   Hi ho, the derrio, the dog takes a cat.

7. The cat takes a rat, the cat takes a rat,
   Hi ho, the derrio, the cat takes a rat.

8. The rat takes a cheese, the rat takes a cheese,
   Hi ho, the derrio, the rat takes a cheese.

9. The cheese stands alone, the cheese stands alone,
   Hi ho, the derrio, the cheese stands alone.